Chester's Fairground

Enjoy the book

[signature]

Chester's Fairground

Lawrence Prestidge

Matador
9 Priory Business Park,
Wistow Road, Kibworth Beauchamp,
Leicestershire. LE8 0RX
Tel: 0116 279 2299
Email: books@troubador.co.uk
Web: www.troubador.co.uk/matador
Twitter: @matadorbooks

ISBN 978 1788039 017

British Library Cataloguing in Publication Data.
A catalogue record for this book is available from the British Library.

Printed and bound by CPI Group (UK) Ltd, Croydon, CR0 4YY
Typeset in 11pt Garamond by Troubador Publishing Ltd, Leicester, UK

Matador is an imprint of Troubador Publishing Ltd

For the Dreamers

Owen Parker   Maria Moy   Toby Phillips

Sophie Snelling   *Zowie Tuff*   *Chester*

'You're mad, bonkers, completely off your head. But I'll tell you a secret. All the best people are.'

Lewis Carroll, *Alice's Adventures in Wonderland*

1

Do you know what gets my goat? Children who don't appreciate what they have. You know the type, those hideous slack jawed children who whinge, moan and kick up a fuss whenever they don't get their own way.

"I want this."

"I want that."

"If you don't get me this I will..."

"Worst day EVER!"

Some of these children believe they have it *tough* because they can't get a limousine to take them to the prom, or because mum won't buy them a new pair of trainers every week. Do these children ever stop to think about the injustice in this world? Do they think of the children who lie sick in hospital beds, do they think of the starving children who dream about a slice of burnt toast or a sprout on Christmas day? Of course not!

Now I personally blame the parents, it was a wise man who said 'the apple never rots far from the tree' and some of these trees could do with chopping down. You know the type of parents I'm talking about, let's think about Harry and Tina Spalding. This lovely couple both go to work every day so their spoilt and pampered children can have everything they've ever dreamed of, Priscilla has her ponies and Callum has four quad bikes and an airgun he uses to terrorise the local cats. Do Callum and Priscilla appreciate their parents? Do they ever think about how hard Tina works scrubbing dishes to pay for her daughter's perm or how long Harry spends in the office so Callum can crash his quad? Of course not but Harry and Tina only have themselves to blame so let's leave them to suffer and think about our story.

This story is about a young man named Owen Parker. Now Owen wasn't one of these beastly children I'm referring to, well not quite. Owen was normally a very kind child who was thankful for what he had. He would help out around the house, peel spuds, put out the bins and he even kept his room tidy...most of the time. Did this mean Owen was perfect?

Of course not! Owen was **OBSESSED** with video games; whether it be shooting zombies, fighting baddies or jumping on mushrooms, Owen loved them all. However there was now only one game he was excited about, one game that he couldn't stop thinking about, one game that occupied every waking moments. The game? '*War Games 5.*'

'*War games 5*' included just about everything a young child could want: explosions, guns, fighting, and all the graphic violence you could handle. It was the type of game that makes mothers shriek and fathers unplug the console.

On the week of its release, Owen was counting down the days to when he would be able to buy the game. And everyone was talking about it at school. By Wednesday, as Owen walked home after yet another boring maths class he decided to take a detour *just* to see the advert in the shop window. But when Owen got there he wished he hadn't. Owen was horrified, he found himself staring at something hideous in that window, it made him dizzy, it made his heart sink, the world around him was coming to an end! The window contained a poster that would break his heart, the poster read '*War Games 5* £59.99'. Owen was shaking in his shoes. This was unbelievable, impossible, inconceivable. Owen got £10

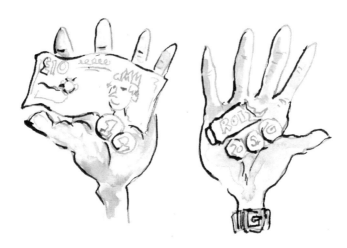

a week and after six weeks of hard saving he had managed to save £11.37 and a half eaten packet of Rolos. He could never afford £59.99 by Friday and there was no way he could wait, just the thought of it made his stomach turn. Owen had to take a deep breath and calm himself. There was only one thing for it, he would have to sweet-talk his parents to get the game he so desperately craved.

Owen marched home, there were three days until '*War Games 5*' was released, so he knew there was no time to spare in terms of convincing his parents. As he walked he thought word for word what he would say to his parents to convince them, rehearsing his speech all the way home.

When he arrived home his parents were preparing dinner.

"Alright sweetie, you're back a bit late today aren't you?" his Mum asked cheerfully as he walked in. Owen didn't respond, he had figured out the perfect pitch to his parents to convince them to give him the money he wanted, and he needed to hit them with it before he forgot it.

"Mum... Dad, there's this new video game coming out in a few days and...."

"No!" his Dad said bluntly, before Owen could continue with his plea.

"What do you mean, no? You don't even know what I'm going to say yet!" Owen cried.

"Owen, you get ten pounds a week and that's it. If there is something you want that's more than that, I suggest you start saving up rather than spending it all on sweets!" his Dad explained flatly. "And before you start; it's no good having a tantrum about it, that will get you nowhere."

Owen knew his Dad would not be convinced so he directed his attention to the weak link: Mum. Owen turned and put on his sad face, lips pouting, eyes imploring, this was the ultimate plea and it had never failed him yet.

His mum looked unimpressed, "don't look at me like that! I agree with your Father, you need to learn how to save your money," she added.

Owen's heart sank, the thought of suffering weeks without playing *'War Games 5'* was just too much to handle. A rage built inside him and his blood boiled. He could feel that he was about to scream at his parents, ready to unleash a torrent of all the times they betrayed him, how they never gave him what he wanted. That time in Blackpool when he couldn't ride the one legged donkey, in Skegness when he wasn't allowed to see the fortune teller, who could really, actually see the future and the time they said he'd have to wait for his birthday present, because it wasn't his birthday! It was clear in Owen's mind that his parents were evil, they hated him and only his suffering made them happy. Just as he was about to unleash his bile and scream at his horrible parents his mum fixed him square in the eye and said: "don't bother shouting, the answer is no."

Owen turned and ran slamming the door in a fit of rage. Red faced and fuming Owen raced down the road, anger followed his every turn as he ran through streets, across roads and bridges. As he ran he found himself more and more tired, slowing the pace and looking around him. Owen stopped. Panting like a dog he looked about and had no idea where he was. "Hmmmm" Owen murmured, "Perhaps I should have planned a route *before* making such a dramatic exit." Owen looked for some kind of clue as to where he might be, there were markings on the road... not very helpful. The houses seemed to be quite new so that meant... not a lot. "Ah ha!" exclaimed Owen "I'm on Pimplethwaite Drive." This was of course true, the sign

told him that, but unfortunately Owen had no idea where Pimplethwaite drive was. He thought it might be near Ramsbottom Crescent or even Scratchybum Gardens but he really didn't know. There was no doubt about it, Owen was lost. However since his parents really 'needed to think about their behaviour' it didn't matter, the longer he left going home the better. He thought to himself. 'Hopefully they'll learn their lesson soon if they think I've run away and will never be coming back.' The only problem was that his stomach was beginning to rumble, Owen was going to have to break into his savings and eat his last Rolo. For now he'd just wander the streets until he worked out where he actually was, then he'd head home and listen to his parents apologise for being so mean.

As Owen slowly wandered the streets, he noticed a man who was having some kind of yard sale outside one of the newer houses. The man was young, maybe sixteen but Owen couldn't really tell. Owen was fascinated by the figure and he couldn't help but notice how incredibly

shy and nervous he looked. His clothes had him almost completely hidden, drowning in a long grey hooded coat his head and face were shrouded by an ill fitting baseball cap. Owen smiled and approached the table where the man had his stuff for sale. He figured that he might as well use his time and, who knows, maybe he could get some directions. It was weird but despite Owen's smile the man would not make direct eye contact with him. Owen shrugged it off and began to examine the table- there were: old records, books and clothes but what really took Owen's eye was a small video game section that was lined up neatly. A lot of the games on the table Owen had already played, most of them he had completed but there was one that caught his attention.

"Chester's Fairground," Owen read out loud before turning it around to look at the back cover. "A fairground like no other. Not for the faint hearted," Owen continued before reacting with, "Cool. Sir, how much is this ga...".

Before Owen could ask his question, he was immediately cut off.

"Completely free… free of charge. You can just take it!" said the man who was looking more nervous than ever and still refusing to meet Owen's eyes.

"Free?" Owen replied with concern. "What's the catch?"

"No catch!" answered the strange man "I've…I've just played the game so…s…so many times… too many times as a matter of fact. I might as well give it away," he added nervously.

"Hmmmm," Owen mumbled, "A free game?" He thought to himself. Maybe today had got better after all. "So what do you do in the game?" Owen asked.

"The cover says it all… experience a fairground like no other. Please…take it," the man replied thrusting his open hands towards Owen in a gesture of dismissal

"And it doesn't cost anything?" Owen checked.

"That's right," the man said, hurriedly waving Owen off once again.

"Okay…" Owen replied before slowly taking the game and walking away down the street. Owen couldn't help turning back to look at the man. He knew something wasn't right about him but he just didn't know what. Owen shrugged then turned his attention back to the case of the game, noticing a line he hadn't seen before which simply said, 'Will Change Your Life Forever'.

"Hey what does this mean?!" Owen called out, but as he turned around to face the man, Owen saw nothing, the houses were all still there but the man, the table and everything on it had disappeared.

Little did Owen Parker know he was about to embark on an experience he would *never* forget.

2

It was getting quite late in the evening when young Owen Parker finally decided that he had taught his parents a lesson and should return home after storming out. At least he now had this video game to play and even if it wasn't '*War Games 5*' it would do for now until they brought that for him. He walked back into the house, expecting his parents to rush to him with pure joy on his return - which of course they should, after all what type of evil parents would refuse their only son his heart's desire? What type of cruel parents would let their only child walk the streets, alone and empty bellied? Yep it was clear that Owen's parents would be so full of guilt they were bound to buy the game, order in a pizza and give him the keys to the cookie jar.

Owen was astounded when he walked in to see them with their feet up, cup of tea in hand watching ballroom dancing on the television.

"Oh hello sweetie, did you have fun?" his mum asked as he entered the living room. Owen was shocked, flabbergasted, he stood open-mouthed as his face flushed in embarrassment, his parents hadn't even broken a sweat! They knew he would come crawling back when he was hungry. Red faced embarrassment was soon replaced by

anger as Owen thought about how unfair his parents had been, about how little they must care for him letting him wander the streets in the dark. Owen clamped his jaw shut and didn't say a word, instead he marched back to his room with his NEW (and FREE) video game.

Peering hard at the front cover of the game Owen couldn't help but notice it seemed weird, not like anything else in his collection, that's what had caught his attention in the first place. Owen couldn't help staring at the strange character that stood in the centre of the box. It was a painting of an old man, or at least old-ish- he couldn't really tell. What Owen did know was that the man on the cover was very odd looking. He was reminded of the Penguin character from Batman. Except he was wearing a red suit with a matching red top hat and bowtie. Apart from a white shirt, everything he wore was red. His smiling face was meant to look friendly but it felt a bit sinister if the truth be told.

Owen got into his room and immediately put the game into the console. As Owen sat down, the game whirred into life. A hideous, cackling laugh came from the TV "Mawahahahahaha," Owen found himself scared as the laugh rang around the room. The TV screen flickered and an image of a fairground appeared on the screen, but it wasn't any fairground you might imagine, this wasn't a place of candyfloss and fun. At first glance there was everything you would expect to see, a ferris wheel, bright lights, stalls and even the obligatory ghost train in the background, but there was something wrong. There was a dark unpleasant feel to it, this certainly wasn't a fairground you would rush to visit.

The game didn't offer many options in the start menu in fact there was only one and that was to START. The top right hand corner of the screen showed four users online. The laugh had shocked Owen but it had just caught him off guard "It must be some sort of horror game," Owen thought to himself. "The guy before clearly couldn't handle it, but it can't be anything worse than I've played already," he thought to himself. It did cross Owen's mind that this might not be the best time to play such a game only a few hours before bed, he didn't want to be too scared to sleep, he did have school tomorrow after all…It took a full three seconds of debate before Owen smashed the button and entered the fairground. The second he did, that repellent laugh, "Mwahahahaha" echoed around his room again. This time though it was as if the laugh came in from inside Owen's bedroom. "Okay, this is weird," Owen thought to himself, but before he could turn to check the room, a light flashed from his screen. It was as if someone had taken a photo directly in his face with the flash on. Owen couldn't see anything, he felt covered in light. Then with a sudden flash, he found himself stood blinking in the middle of a strange street.

Owen moved to the pavement and tried to take in his surroundings before reading the hand painted sign directly in front of him:

Owen couldn't believe his luck. He felt like he had found the most AWESOME video game in the world. He thought it must be some kind of virtual reality game. "WOW! I must have got one of the handful of copies of this game in the world!" he said aloud. This must be some sort of prototype of a virtual fairground he thought. He was surprised he hadn't heard of it before, after all he read about all the latest games. The only conclusion was that this was a beta testing version, Owen couldn't wait to tell his mates about this.

Who needs War Games 5?! he thought to himself. He could now spend the evening on a few rides completely free of charge and decide how to get his parents to buy 'War Games 5' later. Just thinking about how selfish his parents were being got him angry but Owen took a deep breath and decided to make the most of the game. There was an abandoned bike next to the sign. Owen thought it must be part of his virtual experience, so he decided to hop on and biked in the direction the sign was pointing.

Owen pedalled along following signs towards the fairground. However it wasn't long before he found himself panting on the same street, looking at the same first sign.

Owen was confused. Very confused and very tired, all this running and cycling was hard work. "This doesn't make any sense!" Owen said aloud as he found himself seemingly biking down the same street over and over again "This must be some video game glitch! No wonder that guy was giving it away for nothing!"

Just when he was about to give up, he heard fairground music coming from the end of the street. Owen hopped off his bike and followed the music. As he neared the end of the street the fairground lights shone all around him, the music was blaring and he could smell the tempting aroma of chips and hot dogs. The odd thing was that there was not one person in sight. Searching the entrance of the fair he couldn't see a single sign of life. Of course that wasn't a problem, all the more rides JUST for him. However there was a problem and it was the same feeling he got when he was viewing the image of the fairground on the TV screen in his bedroom. Everything looked normal but it *felt* strange.

Owen cautiously walked through the entrance and into the fair. The music continued to play. The smells really were delicious but the rides were dead and the stalls empty. Owen's eyes searched the coasters, the amusements and the food stalls, but still saw no one. The further into the park he went the more the sense that something was wrong grew.

Suddenly hearing voices, Owen turned the corner and saw a small group of children standing next to a merry-go-round. The group consisted of two boys and two girls. Owen slowly approached them before asking, "What's going on? How come there isn't anyone around here? Wait... are you guys real, or are you characters?" Owen felt like this was a very important question to ask, after all there was no point wasting time talking to NPCs characters when he could be jumping on the rides. 'Actually', Owen thought 'the rides might not be so much fun on my own maybe I should just...'. His thoughts trailed off as a glamorous looking girl of about 10 years old approached Owen with a diamond encrusted phone clutched in her hand. Saying nothing she stood next to Owen brandished her phone in the air and aimed it towards herself and a very confused looking Owen.

"Say selfie!" the girl called out as she took a picture. "I don't really know what's real right now!" she said, finally answering him. "There I was walking home and texting my friends and I guess some new app popped up on my phone asking me to try out this new game. I clicked it then the next thing I know I'm right here!"

A grotesquely fat boy, eating a packet of crisps, waddled forward. Not only was this boy a bit of a porker, he also smelt very bad, even amongst the scent of hotdogs and fried doughnuts his stench was overpowering. 'Does this kid ever shower?' Owen wondered.

Before speaking, the large boy started licking bits of crisps off his sausage fingers. "I was at Mr McNulty's sweet shop up on Addison Road and on my way home I found this old video game in an empty pizza box. When I got home I decided to try the game out. After a while, I ended up in front of a sign advertising a completely free Fairground! I didn't really want to walk all the way here but the chance of getting free popcorn, chocolates, toffee apples and candy floss was too good to turn down!" he gabbled.

Owen turned; his attention was drawn to the meanest-looking girl he had ever seen. Hair scraped back to her head, earrings like hula hoops she stood glowering with her arms folded, her brow was furrowed and Owen was convinced she was snarling like a wolf. Her gaze caught his and Owen tried to look away; her eyes were boring into his soul. He didn't want to speak to her but he was too scared to not. Owen's mind whirled in fear, his mouth opened and he was speaking before he had chance to stop himself. Instead of

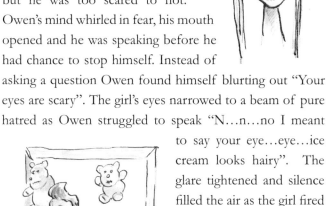

asking a question Owen found himself blurting out "Your eyes are scary". The girl's eyes narrowed to a beam of pure hatred as Owen struggled to speak "N…n…no I meant

to say your eye…eye…ice cream looks hairy". The glare tightened and silence filled the air as the girl fired death rays. Owen looked away, a narrow escape from death.

The last boy in the group rested himself on one of the stalls that surrounded them, unlike the rest of the group he seemed calm, not bothered in the slightest.

"How about you?" Owen asked hesitantly.

"Just like you, man, no idea. I was in the town arcade killing some zombies. Then I see this new arcade game I've never seen before. I go to play it and that's how I ended up with all you losers."

"So we're the only people here and all this is ours to do as we please?" Owen felt the situation was far too good to be true, this guy seemed pretty cool and, even if he did need to share the fairground with those eyes, he could have a good time on the coasters.

"Looks like it!" said the boy leaning back against the stall.

"Let me tweet about this!" shouted the phone-girl. She typed rapidly. "Hashtag-Free Fair!" she yelled excitedly.

Suddenly the music and lights of the fair all stopped and a large spotlight hit the five startled children.

An excited voice boomed out into the silence.

"BOYS AND GIRLS! WELCOME TO CHESTER'S FAIR! HERE FOR ONE NIGHT ONLY. EVERYTHING IS FREE! WE MUST BE CRAZY! SO PREPARE FOR A NIGHT YOU'LL NEVER FORGET! NOW INTRODUCING YOUR HOST … HERE'SSSSSSSSSSSSSSSS CHESTER!"

The merry-go-round alongside them slowly began to move, gaining speed as the lights switched on around it. The music jarred into action as the speed increased and a grinning man appeared on one of the horses.

"But no one was on it!" the fat boy gasped.

The man on the merry-go-round had a white shirt on but other than that he was completely clothed in red. He wore a red blazer, a red tie, a red top hat, smart red trousers

and even his very smart shiny shoes were red. It was the man from Owen's game cover!

"Whoa boy," the man said to the horse on the merry-go-round as the attraction came to a sudden stop. The man hopped off and approached the five children.

"Ta-Da!" the man said as he took a bow.

The children looked at him but were stunned to silence, even the eyes had stopped sending death threats and now showed surprise, with just a hint of anger.

"I was actually expecting a round of applause there... But whatever," the man muttered. "Welcome one and all to Chester's Fairground my little friends! My very own creation, a fair like no other!"

The angry girl grunted to herself before Chester swooped his head towards her.

"You, my beautiful little urchin, please share your thoughts with the whole group."

"I've been to loads of fairs. This is just like all the others. It's certainly not special," spat the girl as she raised an eyebrow and narrowed her eyes at Chester.

Chester started a high pitch giggle at the girl- the laugh got stronger and stronger until it ended in that horrible "Mwhahahahaha" deep cackle Owen had heard before. The children all looked at each other, bewildered.

"Oh I'm sorry my little friends. I promise you'll get it later. You'll laugh; trust me," explained Chester.

"How can you say this fair isn't special? Look at it! No one else is here. We've got this whole place to ourselves! It's ours for the taking!" the cool looking boy said excitedly.

"Precisely!" answered Chester. "I like you already. But first, my little friends, I think it's about time we got more acquainted. Don't you?"

3

"Line yourselves up!" Chester shouted as the five children reluctantly followed his instructions. "Come on stand up straight, don't slouch!" Chester inspected the children like a military general with his troops. The children slowly drifted into line as Chester marched up and down like a disappointed general.

Clapping his feet together in mock salute Chester first approached the chubby boy. Standing face to face with the him, he was greeted with a burp to his face. Chester didn't flinch or turn away he simply stuck out his tongue to taste the burp which had floated in his direction.

"Prawn cocktail. Very nice," Chester said with a smile as he placed a mint in the hand of the porky child. "So you must be Toby Phillips. Don't you just look really faaaaa... bulous and I must say smell really...really ba...ba....b...e....a utiful."

"Where are the free snacks?" Toby belched.

"All in good time. All in good time my wonderful boy, now eat up!" Chester said, closing

23

the boy's fat fist over the mint before moving briskly on to the next child in the line-up.

He stopped in front of the selfie-queen, but clearly couldn't help himself looking back at Toby in disgust. As Chester turned back to face the girl what he actually saw was the screen of her mobile and a flash as the girl grinned and pouted to catch her best side.

Looking more like a confused trout than a pretty 10 year old she gripped Chester close and shouted: "Say selfie!"

The flash fired again and Chester briskly backed away from the girl. "And you are?"

"Maria Moy! A.K.A the queen of selfies!" Maria said proudly.

"Delighted to meet you, your highness. You must be quite the photographer," Chester said. "I must say though that does look quite the mobile phone you have, does it launch missiles, make coffee or run space stations?"

Maria rolled her eyes at Chester's lack of knowledge.

"Of course not! But it's the latest, most up to date mobile in the world," she boasted. "You should get one."

"That's definitely worth considering- wow, in fact I just did... no," said Chester. "Mine's better anyway," He continued, with a smirk.

"Impossible."

"Fine. I'll show you." Chester peeled open his red tailed coat and reached into the inside pocket. His hand burying deeper and deeper inside, rummaging and fishing for something as his face twisted in confusion. "Well that's the strangest thing, I'm sure I put it here somewhere," he said as he rifled and rummaged further.

The children looked on as he pulled out all sorts of strange objects from his pocket – a pocket watch, a rubber duck, a telescope, a boiled egg, a dice, a horn, a teddy bear head, a compass, balloons, a pair of pliers and an apple which he proudly declared was his "old apple phone".

"Ah-Ha!" Chester finally announced removing his gloved hand from the pocket. The hand was shaped into a phone. His little finger was the speaker and his thumb was the receiver. "There we are." Chester showed it proudly.

All the children looked at each other in bewilderment.

Maria rolled her eyes. "Are you kidding me? Do you think I'm really stupid?"

"No. Not *really* stupid," Chester answered.

"That's just your hand." Maria sighed.

"Your powers of observation continue to impress," Chester said. "If you don't believe me, then watch." Chester's three middle fingers started to wiggle and he rested his head on his 'mobile'.

Suddenly Maria's phone started to ring. Her eyes grew huge as she looked at her phone in disbelief. She slowly answered as Chester smirked at her.

"Hello...?" she said hesitantly.

"Told you so!" Chester said before hanging up.

All the children looked at each other in disbelief. They'd never seen anything like that before.

As shocked as Maria was, she was determined to prove her phone was better, after all her phone was her pride and joy.

"Is that all your phone does? Call people?" said Maria with an unimpressed tone. "I have Siri on my phone so it answers any questions I ask it. Do you have Siri?"

"No," answered Chester.

"I thought not," said Maria mockingly.

"But I have Gary!" Chester said.

"Gary? There's no such thing."

"Sssshhhh, he'll hear you," whispered Chester. "Watch this," he added as he raised his 'phone' to his mouth. "Gary, give me one word to describe Maria Moy's personality," he said to his phone.

There was a long pause as the children all once again looked at each other, puzzled.

Suddenly a tinny voice came from somewhere inside Chester's hand. "Hmmmmm," a voice echoed, "I would personally say that Maria Moy is vain".

"Just as I suspected. Thanks Gary." Chester smiled. "See!" he said proudly as he turned his attentions to Maria.

"That's not possible!" said Maria in shock.

"You would think so wouldn't you," murmured Chester.

"Go on ask it something else!" the other boy next to Maria shouted.

"Certainly not! I'm sure Gary has other things to be getting on with and besides I wouldn't want to waste the battery now would I?" Chester turned his attention to the cool boy. "Now hold on, let me guess. You must be Zowie Tuff?"

"Yeah man, everyone online knows the name #Zowie_ Tuff but how do you know it?" Zowie asked.

"How do I know your name?" laughed Chester. "Aren't you the boy with no fear? Spends all his time watching

27

movies that are far too old for him and playing violent video games on his egg box?"

"Nah it's…"

"It's what?"

"An Xbox"

"It used to be a box? What is it now?"

"No it's a…"

"An ex-box I got that but…"

"Never mind," muttered Zowie.

Chester approached Zowie and began to murmur quietly to him. "Rumour actually has it…. that you are afraid of nothing? Rumour also says that there is no video game you haven't played and nothing you have not blasted or mangled: true? Rumour has it you are in fact a virtual legend."

"You got it, YOLO," answered Zowie.

Chester paced back from Zowie looking rather confused.

"YOLO? Oh yes, I had a wooden one but the string snapped."

"Nah man, that's a yo yo, they're naff. I mean Y.O.L.O."

"What's that?"

"You only live once," sighed Zowie. "Everyone knows that."

"Interesting…" murmured Chester. "Thanks for clearing that up. There was me thinking we all lived twice," said Chester as he dismissively moved onto the next child.

Chester now confronted the angry looking girl and her venomous eyes. She stood arms folded, staring daggers into Chester's eyes. "I just love the sweet loving faces of children."

"Don't you know who I am?" growled the angry looking girl.

"Oh yes! Of course. Sophie Snelling. The meanest and toughest girl in Ditherington High School by all accounts. Absolutely delighted to have you here!" Chester answered.

"Exactly. The meanest, toughest girl in school," Sophie said fiercely.

There was a slightly awkward pause as Chester and Sophie faced each other.

"And…?" Chester said.

"Well, don't you care?" Sophie asked.

Chester grinned his pearly white teeth at Sophie and said, "Would it make you feel better if I said I cared for a second… But I got over it?"

Sophie glared and grunted at Chester without saying a word.

"I must ask though. It's been on my mind for a while now. You constantly bully others, so I'd love to know your secrets," Chester said.

"My secrets?" Sophie replied, confused.

"Yes. You must tell me just how perfect you are." Chester received no response from the grumpy girl. "All-righty then..." Chester said as he moved to Owen, who was last in line.

"Last but by no means least then must be Owen Parker," Chester announced as he looked down at Owen. "My sources tell me you ran away from home earlier? May I ask why?"

"My parents hate me. That's why," Owen answered.

"Good heavens!" gasped Chester. "How so?"

"They are always treating me unfairly," Owen muttered.

"Please elaborate my dear boy. When did they last treat you so unfairly, oooh, perhaps we need to inform the police?"

"Well I wanted a new video game. My parents wouldn't get it for me. I think they enjoy seeing me unhappy, I think it was a joke for them. I never ask for much," Owen said, really feeling the injustice.

"How tragic," mocked Chester.

"But it's okay. Because if they hadn't have been so unreasonable I wouldn't have found this neat new game would I. Are you the creator? I must say the graphics are amazing! Wait, how do you know all these things about us?"

Chester tapped his nose twice, strolled a few paces back and observed the five children once again. "Well what a lovely bunch you all are," Chester said with a false smile. "I'm sure we are all going to have a wonderful time tonight. As you all know by now this fairground is completely at your disposal. I want you all to have a night you will never forget. But first things first. It's time to hook a duck!"

4

Chester led the group to a tent in the fairground. Inside the dingy tent was a small pond of dirty water with a selection of tatty looking rubber ducks floating aimlessly around.

"Voila!" Chester shouted proudly. "Aren't they the cutest little ducks you have ever seen? I breed them up here."

"This sucks, why do we have to do hook a duck?" complained Zowie. "Can't we go on a roller coaster or something instead?"

"This is so boring..." Maria sighed.

"Come on children, you know what they say. When life gives you lemons...?"

"Make lemonade," Owen said in a dull tone.

"Make lemonade?" Chester sounded confused. "I always thought it was... when life gives you lemons... squeeze them into people's eyes and make them miserable... but hey your version sounds a lot nicer. Anywhoooo... who shall we have first?"

None of the children was inspired to put a hand up.

"Ah Maria! I saw your hand go up there and, as they say, ladies first." Chester turned his attention to Sophie. "I'll make an exception for you," he whispered.

Chester handed Maria a rod. "Cast away!" bellowed Chester and Maria reluctantly attempted to use her rod to catch one of the ducks.

"Isn't this exciting?" Chester muttered to Owen. "The suspense is killing me."

Maria hooked her rod onto a blue rubber duck and pulled it towards them. "I got it! I got it!" Maria cried. "What do I win? A new phone?"

"Who said anything about winning something?" Chester asked. "We're going to find out what the ducks say about you of course."

"What on earth are you talking about?" asked Maria.

"Oh sorry. Didn't I explain? Don't you know? Ducks are excellent judges of character," Chester declared as he looked at the bottom of the blue duck. "Hmmm, very interesting," he muttered to himself.

"Well, what does it say about me?" Maria asked.

"You really want to know?" Chester said with a smirk.

"Yes!" Maria shouted.

"Okay, as you wish… well…" Chester said hesitantly. "This girl is guilty of being incredibly self-obsessed, viciously vain, hugely narrow minded and deeply shallow. She is completely obsessed with her phone to the extent that she thinks a sunrise is a camera setting. This technology has all but killed any imagination this girl had in that empty head of hers and she will most likely end up in the fast food industry," Chester read out.

"It doesn't say that!" Maria shouted. "You couldn't even fit that all in on the bottom of that duck!"

"I beg your pardon miss but I am not a liar!" Chester retorted. "It does say such things… See?" Chester flashed the bottom of the duck and quickly turned it away again, making it impossible for Maria to see anything.

"Wow! Now that's buzzing, can you make it tell our futures?" asked Zowie.

Chester chuckled to himself. "Of course not my dear boy! They're rubber ducks!" Chester tutted and casually threw the duck back into the pond.

Zowie ran forward and grabbed a rod. "I'm gonna have to try this," he said eagerly.

Easily hooking an orange duck and steadily guiding it towards himself. He grabbed it and went to turn the duck over only to have his hand slapped by Chester's cane. Chester snatched the duck and began to read.

"Zowie Tuff - is in danger in turning into a rather violent child. He watches movies and plays video games far too graphic for his fragile little mind. No good behaviour can come of this," Chester read out.

"That's just a load of rubbish!" laughed Zowie

"We'll see," said Chester with a smirk as Sophie barged her way forward to pick up a rod.

Sophie hooked a pink duck and guided it towards her. She shoved Chester away as she looked at the back of it. After reading it to herself she grunted, a scowl descended and she threw away the duck in anger.

"You continue to make a great impression," said Chester. "Anywhoooo... Owen; you're up."

Owen nervously stepped forward and grabbed a rod. There was something drawing him to a light blue duck. In fact the light blue one was the only one of its kind in the pool. After a few attempts Owen

hooked his rod onto it and slowly pulled it in. He sent it to the outstretched hand of Chester who then turned the duck over and began to read. "Astonishing," Chester muttered as he read. "Absolutely astonishing."

"What is it?" Owen asked.

"Hmmm." Chester pondered. "If you don't mind Owen. I think I'd rather keep this to myself for now. But don't worry... all will be revealed. Right!" He clapped his hands. "Shall we be moving on?"

"What about me?" cried Toby.

"Oh yes of course! Please go right ahead," said Chester as Toby approached him and grabbed a rod.

Chester had to grab a peg that was attached to the top of the tent and put it on his own nose to block Toby's odour. "Ahhh. That's better," he said.

Toby hooked on to a bright yellow duck and dragged it forward to Chester who looked at the bottom of it.

"Well? What does it say?" Toby said eagerly.

Chester looked Toby squarely in the eyes and bluntly said, "You should go on a diet."

The other children looked at Toby awkwardly but he didn't seem fazed at all. He just shrugged his shoulders. He had been told much worse. The other children seemed more embarrassed for him, well at least Owen did, Sophie was back in death stare mode, Maria was doing her hair and Zowie was trying to look cool.

"Right," cried Chester as he clapped his hands once more. "Where to next?"

"CANDY FLOSS!" bellowed Toby as he ran towards a candy floss machine.

Chester rolled his eyes in annoyance.

5

Toby Phillips had never run so quickly. He had dreamt about moments like this. He darted towards the candy floss machine and gazed like a love sick puppy — rubbing his sausage-like fingers all over it. There was an on/off lever and two big buttons, one red and the other green.

"How does it work?" Toby said in a rush. This was the most energy and emotion he had shown since he arrived, actually it was the most energy he'd ever shown, his PE teacher would have been thrilled. Toby had no interest in physical activity and the only time he did anything in PE was when he ate the basketball thinking it was a giant orange.

Chester and the others gathered round the machine as Toby was stood drooling at the thought of the sugary goodness.

"I'll have you know this candy floss machine is the only one of its kind," Chester said proudly.

"How so?" asked Owen.

"You see the

buttons there? The green one will give us enough candy floss for all to share and as much as we wish to have. The red one on the other hand would give out all the candy floss to one person. So the machine lets you share as much as you want with a group of friends or could give one person enough candy floss for... well, who knows?" Chester explained.

"Wow! Get in!" Zowie shouted. "Come on Toby; share it out!"

"You must be joking!" Toby laughed as he grabbed a candy floss stick.

"Oh the shock, I may have to compose myself." remarked Chester.

"Free candy floss is a dream!" Toby shouted.

"Toby, I must warn you. I'm not entirely sure how this will play out!" Chester warned.

It was too late. Toby had pressed the red button and candy floss rushed out of a pipe directly onto Toby's stick. Toby scoffed and scoffed away at the candy floss as it poured out without stopping.

"You greedy pig!" Maria shouted.

"There's enough candy floss there for all of us and then some!" Owen cried.

"I'm in heaven!" cried Toby as he threw the candy floss stick away and put the pipe over his mouth so the candy floss poured straight into his mouth. After what had seemed hours of watching Toby stuff himself like a candy floss teddy bear, he finally resigned.

"Okay. I think I'm full now." Toby chuckled after moving his mouth off the pipe. The candy floss continued pouring out onto his face. "I said I'm done now," Toby cried to Chester but the candy floss continued to flow like a pink river pouring onto his body; covering him from head to toe.

"Turn it off!" Toby shouted as be began to disappear in a pink cocoon.

"When will it stop?" Owen asked Chester.

"I'm not too sure my boy. He wanted all the candy floss for one... So... he's got his own candy floss party going on."

Candy floss now completely covered Toby's body. He looked like a candy floss boy – a very fat candy floss boy. Toby tried to get away but he kept slipping on and falling on the candy floss that surrounded him.

The candy floss seemed to rush out faster and faster until Toby soon found himself cocooned inside a candy floss ball that just kept growing larger and larger by the second. Soon Toby was trapped in the giant ball of candy floss. As the ball continued to grow and grow Chester and the rest of the children had to step back so they weren't consumed by it.

Finally the machine stopped and Owen and the rest of the children stepped back in amazement.

"Anyone for candy floss?" asked Chester awkwardly.

"He's trapped!" Owen shouted in horror.

"He's never going to get out of there!" Zowie gasped.

"Oh he'll get out," Chester assured. "Eventually."

Chester approached the mountain of candy floss and made a hole in its side as big as he could. "Toby I hope you can hear me!" Chester shouted through it. "You need to keep eating your way through the candy floss. It may take a few months... But you'll get out in the end! Anyway... at least it's free, hey?" he added before turning his attention to the other children. "There we are. No harm done. Could have been worse."

"Worse? How could it be worse?" cried Maria

"Well... He could have been trapped in a mountain of cat poo. Imagine eating your way out of that! Anyhoo.... Unless anyone is hungry; let's make haste!"

6

Chester led the four remaining children through the fair.

Zowie noticed a high striker which he couldn't resist having a turn on.

Now if you don't know the high striker it is also known as a strength tester, or the strongman game. The aim is pretty simple, you whack a peg with a massive hammer and try to ring the bell at the top of the machine. These things are the favourites of overweight dads and wannabe bodybuilders.

There were fifteen levels on this particular attraction which meant it would have been a challenge for anyone. Zowie stepped up and hit as hard as he could, only to get a score of three.

"Three? Pah! This thing's busted!" Zowie shouted, throwing the hammer to the floor in disgust.

"Wimp! Give it here." Sophie laughed as she picked up the hammer.

Sophie stepped up to the attraction, confidently raised the hammer high over her head and smacked it down with a great crash. There was no doubt she hit it much harder than Zowie but received a score of only one.

"The stupid thing's broken!" complained Sophie.

"Do you think so?" Chester questioned. "Hold on; let me try," he said as he picked the hammer up in one hand.

Chester looked at the attraction and then softly tapped the hammer on to it.

The levels on it shot up and hit the level fifteen, causing the bell on top to ring. "Seems to be working fine."
"How can it be?" asked Maria. "You didn't hit it hard enough."

"My dear child, there are different types of strength," explained Chester. "Anyhooo, we had best be moving on."

7

Chester led the group across the deserted fairground to a mirror maze that sat proudly in the heart of the fair.

"Ahhhh, the Mirror Mirror Maze. One of my finest attractions," Chester said.

"Don't you mean mirror maze?" Owen asked, puzzled.

"No. Mirror Mirror Maze. That's why I said it," said Chester.

"Finest attraction? Are you kidding me? Mirror mazes are dumb, boring and *so last century!*" whined Maria. 'They're easy, all you do is walk around.'

"As I said…" Chester sighed too. "It's a mirror mirror maze and hey if it's so easy, please go ahead and show us all."

"No problem," Maria said confidently. "Let me just take a selfie by the entrance before I go in." She raised her phone high above her head.

Suddenly Chester grabbed Maria's phone and launched it into the air.

"Ooooops... I appear to have dropped your phone. Butter fingers."

"My phone!" Maria shrieked. She looked absolutely devastated by the loss of her phone, it was as though she was grieving the loss of a close friend. "What am I supposed to do now?"

"I know, I do wonder how humanity could ever survive without the use of mobiles," Chester remarked jeeringly.

"Well I couldn't possibly go in the maze now," said Maria.

"Why on earth not?" snapped Chester.

"How am I supposed to find my way out of the mirror maze without my GPS?"

Chester covered his face with his hand to hide his frustration. "Just get in the maze."

Maria entered the maze hesitantly.

"Come on then. We may as well move on," said Chester.

"She's going to be in that maze for quite some time. Lead on McDuff!" Chester shouted as he pointed at Zowie.

8

Maria Moy slowly made her way into the Mirror Mirror Maze, still grieving the loss of her phone.

At first all the mirrors showed nothing but a normal reflection of Maria as she made her way in. Of course she stopped to check her hair was straight, adjust her dress, practice her pout and try a few poses before moving on. As she got deeper in the reflections began to shift, beginning to show her in different shapes.

Maria went from enormously fat in one mirror to looking incredibly thin in another. She continued to walk

through the maze seeing her reflection form different shapes in each mirror.

This is *exactly* like a mirror maze, she thought. Obviously she didn't enjoy the experience but at least her hair still appeared to be straight.

As Maria slowly ventured further into the maze, the mirrors suddenly started acting rather strangely. In one she saw herself trapped inside a mobile phone. It couldn't be a real reflection but it looked so real. The image was moving, looking visibly upset as she tried to break free from it. Maria found the image upsetting, the hopelessness of this prisoner trying to break free left her feeling the same: hopeless.

Maria couldn't bear to look anymore so she quickly moved on.

She was even more shocked by what she saw in the next mirror. There she was, a little girl playing in the mirror. Her teddies were all around her and she sat bandaging them nursing them better, checking their little teddy heartbeats with her plastic stethoscope. A tear began to run down her face. In this image Maria saw all the hopes, dreams and innocence she had as a little girl. A memory that had been lost for years returned, she wanted to be a doctor when she grew up. Of course that was the young Maria before the arrival of the selfie queen.

The images shifted now showing Maria older, sat applying makeup, brushing her hair obsessing with her phone. All her dreams and passion had disappeared as Maria grew older. She had become obsessed with phones and social media. She had become obsessed with how she looked to others and had forgotten her dreams.

A ghostly image of Chester wild eyed, dressed in red and with his long coat flapping in the wind appeared in the mirror looking at Maria, suddenly the entire maze was covered with the same ghostly image.

"Don't be anything less than everything you can be," they all said in unison.

Over and over again the images of Chester repeated it. "Don't be anything less than everything you can be."

The mirrors closed in on Maria and the maze began to

cave in towards her. Everywhere she turned and ran, she saw images of Chester coming in closer to her. Soon she was confined to a tiny square. She started feeling dizzy, and the room and images looked like they were spinning.

Maria fell to the floor, the tiles span as she dropped and she felt herself falling, falling for what seemed like an eternity. She had blacked out.

Maria woke up panicked and spluttering, she was trapped, surrounded on all sides. As she began to thrash in her prison she saw that she was surrounded by plastic balls. Small multi-coloured plastic balls were everywhere she looked. She realised she was safe - confused - but safe, Maria began to breathe again.

9

Chester waded on through the fair with Zowie Tuff, Sophie Snelling and Owen Parker.

"Why are we leaving Maria in there?" Owen asked. "Will she be all right?"

Chester ignored Owen's question.

"What if both Toby and Maria end up dead? Wouldn't that be cool?" Zowie said excitedly.

Chester continued to ignore them as he strode on purposefully.

"I think it's about time you explained yourself to us! What kind of weird video game is this!" demanded Sophie.

Chester suddenly stopped moving and turned to face the children. "Sometimes you don't need explanations. It is what it is. Now let's continue. If I had a penny every time I was asked to explain myself I would have exactly seven pound and seventy-seven pence, now isn't that something?" Sophie looked confused as Chester continued without looking back, the children followed without enthusiasm.

The group now found themselves stood outside a very dark and ugly looking attraction. The outside of the ride looked like something you might see in a horror movie.

Devil red eyes were painted all over it, and dangerous-looking spikes and cages were scattered around the entrance – which was a giant devil's mouth complete with a forked tongue and spiky teeth and a big sign saying:

ADULTS ONLY

"What's that?" Sophie said as she pointed to the devil's head.

"Ah! I thought this might spark some interest," Chester declared. "What you are seeing is in fact the scariest ghost train in the world. I call it, 'The Tunnel of Terror'."

"Have you been on it?" Sophie asked.

"Absolutely…not," Chester answered. "I got this ride given to me by the Bogeyman. He couldn't wait to get rid of it."

"The Bogeyman?" asked Owen puzzled.

"Yes, the Bogeyman. He has his own horror park in Transylvania. I've never seen him wanting to give something away so much. But no, I will never go on it. No one who rides on it ever seems to come off the same."

"What's that?" Zowie asked, pointing to a lever. Alongside the lever were four levels that read—

"Ah! Well spotted. These are the different levels of terror you can experience on the ride. No one ever goes above the first," answered Chester.

"Count me in!" Zowie shouted as he approached the attraction.

Chester blocked him with an outstretched arm. "I'm afraid I can't let you do that Zowie as the sign says this is strictly **ADULTS ONLY**."

"Mr. Do you know who you are talking to?" sneered Zowie with an eyebrow raised.

"Please... do remind me," answered Chester.

"Look mate, I do what I want, I play video games I

shouldn't. I watch movies I shouldn't, there's nothing that scares me, not one bit. I'm fearless! And nobody tells me what I can and can't do," Zowie shouted as he ran towards the attraction.

"I highly advise against this…" Chester said rather unconvincingly.

Zowie ran closer to the attraction and shocked everyone when he pulled the lever all the way down to **'ARE YOU NUTS'**, hopped on to one of the karts and disapeared into the darkness of the devil's mouth.

"Chester, is Zowie going to be okay?" Owen asked with genuine concern.

"I think that ship sailed long ago…" Chester said with a rather blank expression.

Chester then turned out of his trance-like manner and

turned his attentions to Owen and Sophie. "And then there were two," he said. "Come on then. Let's keep moving on," he said as they walked on through the fair.

10

Zowie sat in his kart and strapped himself in, despite there being no one there the ride seemed to know exactly when Zowie was ready and the kart lurched forward and into the 'The Tunnel of Terror'.

Spooky music was playing as he went in. It was pitch black apart from the glow of the dark plastic ghosts, bats and vampires.

"Is this it?" Zowie laughed to himself. "This is a joke!"

The ride rattled along until there was a sudden and almighty drop! Zowie's stomach lurched and as the kart levelled off he laughed at himself for being caught by surprise. The kart continued rattling along and as they descended deeper and deeper it seemed to get hotter and hotter.

Suddenly out of the darkness Zowie saw silhouettes of three bodies coming towards him. They were completely covered in a bright, fiery red glow that shimmered and dripped into the darkness below. It was as if these bodies had been dunked in bright red paint. Zowie scoffed at them but as they got closer he could see they had no faces.

The bodies encircled Zowie's kart. They didn't touch him, but continued to circle the kart again and again, dripping and hissing at the now petrified Zowie.

"Okay Chester, very good, I want to get out now," said Zowie trying to hide the panic in his voice. "Chester, let me out!"

The bodies around him circled faster still hissing and laughing as Zowie lost the last of his bravery.

Zowie shut his eyes hoping it would all stop but as he did the kart jolted forward and began to gain speed. Faster and faster the kart rattled on as the red bright bodies faded behind him.

Once again surrounded by darkness Zowie could see nothing, but he could hear voices. The noise was almost deafening and it sounded like the cries of thousands of people, cries for help mingled with taunts and jeers directed at Zowie.

The kart suddenly came to a halt and Zowie was still, he could see nothing but was sure there was space like a chasm or huge pit beneath him. The cries had stopped and all Zowie could hear was the sound of a breeze. The temperature dropped and Zowie felt like he was outside during winter. He curled himself in a ball in the kart and started to shake from the bitter cold. Out of the gloom a blue figure appeared in front of him. Icy blue.

It appeared to be the figure of a woman— but she was completely covered in a glowing light and it was impossible to make out her face. There was a feeling of sorrow about this figure. Zowie couldn't make out why but he knew this figure was desperately sad. A cold frosty tear started to run down his face as her sadness consumed him leeching into his very bones and chilling his heart. The figure slowly unfurled her light blue hand and placed her finger on Zowie's tear.

Zowie's face was overtaken with a burning sensation of danger and he flung himself backwards in the seat to get away from her touch.

As he did the blue face suddenly changed, twisting and contorting into a hideous green, demonic face. Its mouth opened and screamed right at him. Zowie felt the kart kick into life and the heat returned.

Faster and faster Zowie sped as he heard the cries from people surrounding him once more. He saw images of war flashing at him through the darkness. They reminded him of his violent games, but he knew they were *very* real. He saw the images of death caused by war, poverty caused by war and families affected by war. Zowie closed his eyes and screamed. He screamed as he never had before.

Suddenly the kart came to a stop. Zowie nervously opened his eyes. He was covered in sweat and shaking, but he was back at the front entrance to the attraction.

Zowie hopped out of the kart as fast as he could and sat down panting heavily-, #Zowie_Tuff was no more.

11

"What an ugly doll!" Sophie snorted as she, Owen and Chester looked on at one of the arcade stalls. "Who would want to win that?" she added pointing towards a particularly ugly rag doll that appeared to have a look of horror on its face.

"Yes. I see what you mean," sighed Chester. "But I can safely say the doll you see there is unique. One of a kind. Nowhere in the world will you see the match of that doll."

"Really?" asked Sophie.

"Now would I lie to you?" Chester smirked.

"I'm going to win it!" Sophie suddenly stated.

"Why would you want that, it's hideous!" Owen asked, puzzled.

"Do you have any idea how much that thing could be worth if it's one of a kind?" Sophie answered.

"It could be one of a kind for a reason..." remarked Chester.

"I bet someone out there would pay hundreds for it... And I'm going to find the sucker that would. Now what do I have to do?" Sophie asked.

"Isn't it obvious?" Chester asked. "All you have to do is stand behind this white line and you get three attempts to throw a ball onto the bullseye of the target," Chester pointed out an archery target a few metres away. It had a rather large red button in the middle where the Bullseye would be.

Sophie grabbed a ball from beside the white line and approached the target.

"Make sure you stay behind the line!" Chester cried. "Cheaters never prosper!"

Sophie sighed and reluctantly stood behind the line. She threw her first ball and just missed the top of the target. She looked back at Chester and Owen and grunted.

She picked up the second ball and eyed the target closely as Chester and Owen watched on.

A noise distracted Owen and he turned to see that Chester suddenly had a bag of popcorn he was munching away at as he and Owen watched. Owen looked at him, thoroughly confused.

"Oh sorry. Did you want some?" Chester asked offering the bag to him.

"Erm sure," answered Owen as he grabbed a handful of popcorn and put it in his mouth. His face twisted, his eyes bulged and he struggled to keep his mouth closed. "What flavour is this?" asked Owen before spitting out what he could.

"Bogey flavoured." Chester smiled. "It's my most popular flavour."

Owen couldn't tell if Chester was being serious or not, but he knew, whatever flavour it was, it was disgusting.

Owen turned to see Sophie stare hard at the target before releasing a powerful overarm lob at the target. The ball looked as if it was heading straight for the bullseye and must have only just missed by an inch.

"That was close," Owen called out.

"Oooh, what a rotten bit of luck!" commiserated Chester. "Oh well, at least you have one more try!"

"This is a scam!" Sophie shouted in anger. "I'm a great thrower and I really would only need one go to hit that stupid thing. I bet you make it move!" she added as she pointed to Chester.

"Yes... I trained it to move," Chester said mockingly.

"Well I've got one more go and you certainly aren't going to con me!" Sophie shouted as she picked up the remaining ball stepped past the line and edged closer to the target.

"Erm…Sophie. I really wouldn't do that," Chester warned.

"I'd listen to him if I were you, think about what happened to Toby and Maria and…"

"Shut up twit!" snarled Sophie who was now standing right in front of the target with the final ball in her hand. Raising the ball up she smashed it down right into the centre of the button marking the bullseye.

As she did confetti started to explode everywhere and a merry sound of trumpets played around them.

"I won! I won!" cried Sophie.

Chester hid his face with his hand as if he knew what was about to happen.

The trumpet sound faded out, and the confetti stopped flowing as there was a sudden silence.

Sophie looked around anxiously. "What's going on?"

"I did warn you." Chester sighed.

"What do you m—" Sophie couldn't finish her sentence. She grabbed her mouth in horror. She was trying to speak but all that came out was a mumble. Her mouth

had suddenly been sewn up, stitches appeared closing the top of her mouth to the bottom. Sophie squirmed in panic as her eyes changed to buttons and she began to shrink.

"I told you not to cheat," Chester said as he looked down at her.

Owen looked down at her and stared in horror. Sophie was now a rag doll. Chester picked up the doll that had once been Sophie Snelling and admired it closely.

Owen was stunned. "That's awful!"

"I know!" cried Chester. "Who on earth in their right mind is going to want to win this! I've never seen such an ugly doll. I'm going to have my work cut out trying to get rid of this one." Chester placed the rag doll on a shelf above the target with the other 'unique' dolls and Sophie seemed to fit right in, she even had that strange look of horror on her face.

Owen looked around and began to feel very nervous, he was the only child left!

12

"Well. I better be going," Owen said.

"Going where?" Chester questioned.

"Well… home, this really has been an incredible game, but I think it's time for me to quit and go have my dinner now," Owen answered.

"I see," muttered Chester.

"Yeah, so I'll be off now, thanks. See you around! Guess I just return to the start right?" Owen said as he turned around, trying to make as quick a getaway as possible. A firm hand placed itself on his shoulder. Owen turned around to look at Chester.

"Just before you go... there is one other thing," said Chester, smiling, as he pointed to a towering rollercoaster ride.

Owen had never seen such a thing in his life, it was huge, monstrous, the rollercoaster to end all rollercoaster's. He could barely see the top, just the thought of it being there was making him nervous, never mind riding the thing!

"You need to try it; it's one of my newest attractions," Chester said as they went through the entrance to the ride.

Owen looked at the seat at the bottom of the ride and then craned his neck to try and catch a glimpse of the top. He couldn't.

"It's one of those rides where you drop down…isn't it?" Owen gulped.

"Sure is," Chester said with a smile.

"Ah, well you see, I'm terrified of heights. So I shouldn't really go on it," Owen said.

"Well, what a perfect way to overcome your fear! Overcome fear and anything is possible." Chester's firm hand guided Owen to the seat and fixed the safety harness over him. Owen knew there was no point resisting, he was trapped.

Owen started to shake with nerves, his stomach was beginning to rebel at just the thought of the drop. There was no way he wouldn't be sick.

"Chester, what was it the rubber duck said about me?" Owen asked as Chester stood at the control panel ready to send Owen to his doom.

"The question is, my dear boy, are you ready to know?" Chester replied.

"Ready as I'll ever be," answered Owen desperately trying to take his mind off the ride.

"Well my boy, your duck did say there was still hope for you. But you are guilty of not appreciating what you have. You are a kind boy and you should be thankful your parents raised you well. But the more you let these horrible video games consume you- the more horrible and real they become. That's why you're here. I think you need to realise just how lucky you are and I have every faith this ride will do just that," assured Chester.

"How?"

"Well, when you get to the top I shall explain all," Chester said before pulling a lever which lifted Owen up higher and higher. Owen swallowed hard and tried to think about something else

Owen closed his eyes as the coaster started to rise. Feeling the clunk and clank of the chains Owen felt as if the journey was taking forever. He wondered just how much longer it would take to reach the top and tried not to think about how long it would take to get down.

Suddenly the ride came to a shuddering halt. Owen opened one eye and gasped as he realised how high up he was. He could see his whole town; he was pretty sure he could even see his house in the distance. Owen was now sure this video game was certainly not all it seemed to be. Owen closed his eyes again and waited a few seconds before daring to open them both.

He peeked directly down below him. His heart leapt into his mouth when he saw how high above the fair he was. It must be two miles down thought Owen, and his stomach shuddered once more.

A voice suddenly burst from a speaker on the front of the coaster.

"Enjoying the view?" Chester's crackling voice asked.

"Can we just get this over with?" Owen cried.

"All righty then. Now Owen, the hope is by the time you get to the floor from the drop you will have had a huge reflection on your life and realise how lucky you are. Simple as that really. Do that and there is no need to panic," explained Chester.

"And if I don't?" asked Owen.

There was quite a long a pause before Chester's voice crackled out of the speaker once more. "We'll get to that if we come to it. Now are you ready?"

"Can you just get me down? How can I get home?" cried Owen.

"Isn't it obvious? All you have to do is clap your heels together three times and say *there's no place like home*," replied Chester.

"Really?"

"No… not really," answered Chester. "Now, after three…"

Owen took a huge deep breath, preparing himself for the countdown.

"THREE!" shouted Chester and Owen plummeted from the sky.

Owen had never travelled so fast. He found himself crushed into his seat. Clutching the harness. Trying to find the breath to scream. He couldn't sit forward, his stomach was in his mouth and when he tried to close his eyes the sheer speed of the ride forced them open. Everything Owen looked at was a blur, but then suddenly images started to appear.

Owen painstakingly turned his head to the left and saw children not much younger than him in hospital beds looking very sick. On his right Owen saw images of children in Africa starving.

Owen began to see images of crying children who never even knew their parents. He saw other heartbroken children whose parents had died. Owen didn't want to look any longer and wanted to turn away, but he couldn't, he had to watch.

Owen saw images of himself and his own behaviour. He was watching how he had spoken to his parents, whenever he hadn't got his own way. He couldn't believe how ungrateful, selfish and nasty he looked. He could see the person his obsession with video games were turning him into. He was no longer scared of the ride around him; he was fixated on the images of himself and his family.

He began to see how hard his parents worked to try

and give him everything they could. He saw images of his parents reacting to the realisation of him running away. He saw the look of worry on their faces; he saw their tears. He began to feel the heartbreak they went through. It was as if someone had kicked him hard in the stomach. All the images around him began to disappear.

All Owen could see once again was the blur of lights. All he began to think of was how much he wanted to be home and see his family.

Suddenly he noticed the ground and the lights of the fair getting closer and closer to him. Owen had no doubt in his mind he was going to hit the floor. He closed his eyes, hoping the impact would be painless.

But then there was a sudden stop and lurch as he was thrown back into his seat

*****

Owen opened his eyes and found himself slumped on the bed. He was back in his room looking at his television, Owen was puzzled as he took in the sights around him. Nothing had changed, that was the strangest thing, nothing had changed; here he was sat on the bed in front of his console and nothing had changed, Owen's mind raced, he sprang forward and turned it off, whatever happened he never wanted to play that game again.

He slowly stood up, bewildered. Had he imagined the whole thing? He had been sleeping late recently. Was it some bizarre nightmare?

Whatever it was, Owen was just happy to be away from that fair.

Owen ran downstairs to his parents who were still watching the ballroom dancing on television. Although

Owen felt he hadn't seen them in hours to them it was as if he had only been home a few minutes

"Dinner isn't quite ready yet Owen," his Mum said as Owen appeared.

Owen gave both his parents a huge hug. There was a sense of relief from all of them which flowed all around the house.

"What's brought all this on?" Owen's Dad asked.

"I'm so sorry if I've been speaking to you guys horribly lately. I didn't mean to storm off like that earlier," he explained.

Both his parents smiled. Although they knew Owen was getting older and was getting to the age where he wanted more things, they knew he was still the thoughtful boy they had brought up. They had a great dinner that evening. It was the first time in a long time they had sat down as a family and talked over dinner: it was a real pleasure. Normally Owen would rush his dinner to go back on his console or watch a TV programme in his room alone. But tonight they all sat together and enjoyed it.

Owen never knew what to make of the game 'Chester's Fairground'. After putting the disc back in its case, it mysteriously vanished the following morning. But it was the eye opener Owen needed.

No matter what reality Chester is in, whether it be in the real world or the virtual world, we all need to stop and think to ourselves - what would the rubber ducks say about me?